Malory

Published in the United States of America and its dependencies by
Oak Tree Publications, Inc.
9601 Aero Dr., Suite 202
San Diego, CA 92123

This edition copyright © Templar Publishing Ltd 1985
Text copyright © Richard Carlisle 1985

ISBN 0-86679-043-8

Library of Congress Cataloging-in-Publication Data

Carlisle, Richard, 1949–
Who's afraid of spiders?

Summary: A child realizes that spiders are not
something to fear after thinking about how very small
they are and how they probably get lonely.
[1. Spiders—Fiction.   2. Fear—Fiction]
I. Anstey, David, ill.   II. Title.
PZ7.C216375Whs   1987   [E]   86-21842
ISBN 0-86679-043-8

This book was devised and produced by Templar Publishing Ltd,
107 High Street, Dorking, Surrey

Color separations by Positive Colour Ltd, Maldon, Essex

Printed and bound by New Interlitho, Milan, Italy.

Dedicated to Maxine and Sam who were never really afraid

WHO'S AFRAID
—— of spiders? ——

Written by Richard Carlisle
Illustrated by David Anstey

Oak Tree Publications, Inc.

San Diego, California

I'm afraid of spiders.
They've got such funny ways.
They quickly flash across the floor,
then disappear for days.

It's that kind of surprising thing
that leads me to believe
a spider seen in late July
comes back on Christmas Eve!

I'm afraid that spiders
might hide above my head,
and when I look the other way
they'll sneak into my bed.

And then when I'm asleep,
they'll nibble at my toes.
And when I'm getting dressed I'll find
one hiding in my clothes.

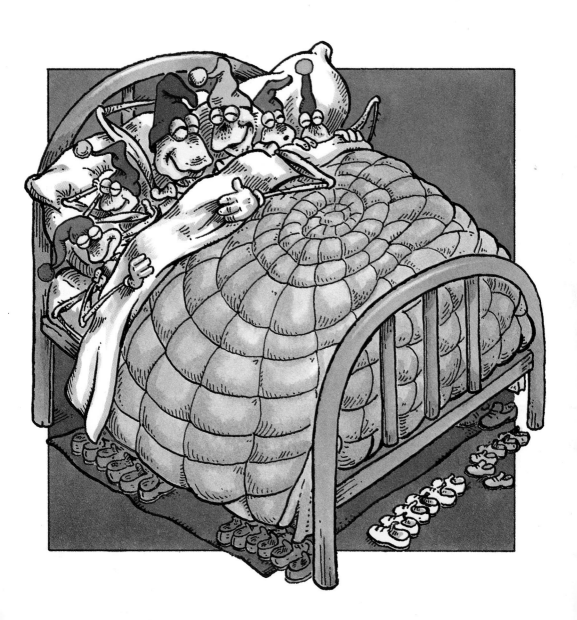

I'm afraid of spiders.
They've got such hairy knees.
They never knock when they come in
and never once say please.

I also think their bodies
are much too fat and round,
and if they run, they never make
a single warning sound.

Spiders are quite speedy
especially when they run.
And though they never smile a lot
they're really having fun.

One spider that I heard about
was tripped up on the floor.
It lost a leg by accident
then simply grew one more.

Once upon a time I'm told,
spiders were like slugs.
They wriggled on their tummies
and looked like legless bugs.

But then it was discovered
that legs gave greater speed.
So spiders started running,
very fast indeed!

They also found that weaving webs
improved their family life.
And lonely spiders found out how
to catch a willing wife.

Webs were good at lunchtime too
since sometimes flies dropped by.
And then they had a pantry
that kept their dinner dry.

And when you think about it,
spiders aren't so bad.
They laugh and cry, and go to sleep,
and sometimes they get sad.

They also have their moms and dads
who sometimes play the fool,
and when they're tiny babies
they go to spider school.

In fact, it really is quite strange
that everyone should fear
a little creature on the run
from over there to here.

Spiders might LOOK nasty,
and make you want to cry.
But think how big you seem to them,
a million inches high.

So if I feel a tickle
at the bottom of my bed,
I won't think it's a spider
but just an itch instead.

And if I see a spider
crawling up my wall,
I'll tell myself it's tiny
while I'm extremely tall.

Mom says they are much more scared
and is it really fair,
that we don't play our games nearby
just because they're there?

Spiders must get lonely too,
and wish they had more friends
to splash about with in the bath
and play with on weekends.

So now when spiders meet me
I never run and hide.
I simply say they can't stay here
then point the way outside.